Then I was trained to pull a carriage. The farmer often drove me in double harness with my mother, for she was able to teach me how to behave. "Lift your feet up well when you trot, and never bite or kick even in play," she told me.

Then one day in May, I was sold to Squire Gordon. As the man came to fetch me, I remember my mother's parting advice. "Do your best, wherever you are, and keep up your good name."

So I came to Birtwick Park and was put into a comfortable loose box. I looked through the iron rails and saw two other horses.

"My name is Merrylegs," said the fat, grey pony in the stall next to mine. Ginger, a tall chestnut mare, stood in the stall beyond.

"What shall we call him?" Squire Gordon asked, showing me to his wife.

"He's as black as ebony and quite a beauty - let's call him Black Beauty," she suggested. Even James, the stable boy, agreed it was a good name.

One day, John the coachman harnessed me to the dog-cart to take the squire into town. It had been raining heavily, but we went along merrily until we reached a bridge over the river. "The river's rising fast," said the man at the toll gate.

Though the water had flooded the road up to my knees in some places, we got through to the town.

The first place that I can remember was a large pleasant meadow with a pond, and shady trees leaning over it.

While I was young I ran by my mother's side in the day time, and at night I lay down close by her.

There were six young colts in the meadow besides me. As I grew bigger I used to have great fun with them and we would gallop round and round the field.

As I grew older and more handsome many people came to admire me. My coat shone black as a rook's wing except for one white foot and a pretty white diamond on my forehead.

When I was four-years-old and quite grown up, the farmer said it was time to break me in. Although he was kind and gentle, I hated having a bit in my mouth, a saddle on my back and being taken to the smith's forge to have iron shoes put on my feet. It didn't hurt as the blacksmith nailed them on, but my new shoes felt very heavy at first.

But the master was a long time about his business and it was dark by the time we approached the bridge again. The moment my feet touched the first part of the bridge I felt sure there was something wrong. "Go on Black Beauty," urged my master, touching me with the whip, but I dare not go forward.

Just then the toll-gate keeper ran out of his house waving a lantern and shouting, "Hey, halloo, stop!"

"What's the matter?" shouted my master.

"The bridge is broken in the middle and part of it is carried away."

We had to take a long detour and it was very late before we reached home. The mistress came out, crying; "Have you had an accident?"

"No, my dear, but if your Black Beauty had not been wiser than we were, we might all have been drowned," said the Squire.

After this, Squire Gordon and his wife decided to visit some friends. The journey was a long one and as darkness fell it was decided that we would stop the night at a hotel.

The ostler led me into the stables while another man brought in Ginger. James watched while we were rubbed down.

Later a young man smoking a pipe came into the stables. "Go up to the loft and get some hay will you?" asked the ostler. "But put that pipe down first."

Shortly after this we settled down to sleep. But within half an hour I was awake again. There was a strange smell in the air and I felt very uncomfortable. The atmosphere seemed thick and choking and I heard Ginger coughing.

The trap door to the loft was open and through it came a crackling
sound that made me tremble all over. Soon all the horses were awake,
pulling at their halters and stamping in fear, as the flames, started by the
forgotten pipe, began to spread. At last the door was flung open and James
came running in. Coughing from the smoke, he took the scarf from around
his neck and tied it lightly over my eyes. Then he led me outside to the
yard.

Then he rushed back for Ginger, but she was too terrified to move. I
let out a shrill whinny and Ginger heard me. Then she and James came out,
just as the stable roof crashed down.

"Stand back! Make way!" cried a voice as two horses dashed into the yard, pulling a heavy fire engine. As we were led away to a safer place, Ginger nuzzled me. "I would never have had the nerve to come out, if I hadn't heard you whinny," she said, gratefully.

James, who had been woken by the commotion in the stables, was praised for his bravery and soon after, when Mrs Gordon's brother was looking for a coachman, James got the job.

We were all sad to see him go, but in his place came little Joe Green, the gardener's boy.

Joe was only fourteen and small for his age, so he had to learn to groom a horse by looking after Merrylegs.

At first the old pony was quite upset. "How would you like to be mauled about by a boy who knows nothing?" he complained. But Joe was eager to please and after two weeks of hard work, Merrylegs said he thought the boy would turn out well.

That day we had been given the run of the orchard, one of our favourite places.

"Let's go down to the other end, I believe the wind has blown down some apples," said Merrylegs, so we raced over the grass and were all soon in good spirits again.

I had been in this happy place for three years when we heard, through talk in the stable, that great changes were to come. The Squire and his wife were to leave to live abroad, and the big house and the horses were to be sold.

Merrylegs was given to the vicar's wife and Joe went to look after him. Then John put the saddle on Ginger and the leading rein on me, and rode us across country to Earlshall Park.

Although this was a much grander place than the Squire's, there was something about it I didn't like.

The Earl and the Lady lived in a very fine house and Mr York, the coachman, was in charge of the stables. John warned him that neither Ginger nor myself had been forced to wear a bearing rein to keep our heads held high.

"I don't hold with it myself," said the coachman. "But her Ladyship always wants to keep up with the fashion, however cruel it may be."

One afternoon, her Ladyship came rustling down the steps in her silk gown, ready to go to a duchess's garden party. "You must put those horses' heads higher, they're not fit to be seen," she cried.

My head was forced up first, but Ginger saw what was coming, and reared up, plunging and kicking wildly. At last she kicked over the carriage pole and fell down. "I knew there would be trouble," said the coachman as he took me to the table and bathed my swollen leg. "And if her Ladyship can't get to the garden party, I can't help it."

They dared not put Ginger in the carriage again and, not long after my leg was healed, the Earl and the Lady went away to London taking the coachman with them.

The younger members of the family stayed in the country and Lady Anne chose me to ride. She called me Black Auster and often rode out with her cousin Blantyre, who was mounted on Lizzie, a thoroughbred bay mare with a lively spirit. Although Lizzie was a bit nervous, one day Lady Anne persuaded her cousin to swap mounts. As we were setting off, a message was brought for Blantyre to deliver to Dr Ashley.

When we reached the doctor's house, Blantyre hitched my reins to the railings outside.

   While we waited, a boy drove several colts out of a nearby field and
one of them bolted across the road, blundering against Lizzie's hind legs.
Frightened, she kicked violently and dashed off down the path in a
headlong gallop.
   I gave a loud, shrill neigh for help. Again and again I neighed until
Blantyre came running to the gate. He sprang into the saddle and gave
chase, catching sight of Lizzie and her rider as she turned onto a rough
common. About half way across was a wide ditch and Lizzie took the leap,
stumbled, then fell.
   "Now Auster, you must do your best," groaned Blantyre, as I too took
the jump.

Face-down and motionless amongst the heather lay my poor young mistress. A man cutting turf had also seen the accident, and as Blantyre knelt beside Anne, he shouted to the other man to ride back for the doctor.

Although he was not a good rider, I carried him as fast as I could to the doctor's house, then to Earlshall Park to summon more help.

Two days later Blantyre came into the stable and told the groom that Lady Anne had recovered. "I'm sure Auster knew the danger she was in," he said. "We must never let her ride any other horse but him."

"Now I can look forward to a happy life," I told myself. But I reckoned without the groom, Reuben Smith, who had been left in charge.

One of the light carriages needed repair and Reuben was told to take

it into the town and ride me back home.
We left the carriage at the makers and
after saddling me, Reuben rode to the
White Lion. There he told the ostler to
feed me well and have me ready by four
o'clock.

But Reuben met some friends at
the inn and stayed drinking with them
until night. Then the ostler pointed out
that a nail had been lost from my shoe,
but Reuben just said, "That can wait
until we get home."

"Have a care, Mr Smith," warned the landlord, but Reuben rode me at
a furious gallop. The road had been newly mended with sharp stones, and I
could feel one of my shoes coming loose. By the time we had reached the
toll gate it was off completely.

Soon my hoof was badly cut by the stones, and I stumbled and fell on both my knees. Reuben fell off and was knocked unconscious, so I limped to the roadside where the soft grass grew.

It was nearly midnight when I heard the sound of Ginger's hooves and I neighed loudly. Then I heard the sound of men's voices as they came to the rescue.

It took a long time for my knees to heal, but the scars still showed. "It's a great pity, but I cannot have knees like that in my stables," said the Earl. "He must be sold." It was a sad parting from Ginger when I had to leave and was sent to be sold at a horse fair.

As I stood in line with some other horses, I had my mouth, eyes and legs examined, then I was trotted up and down to show my paces. One man spoke gently, while another buyer was hard-looking and loud-voiced.

Just as I feared the second one was closing the deal, the first one returned and made a higher bid.

My new owner was Jerry Barker, who drove a cab in London. He lived in a small house with his wife Polly, and his two children Lucy and Dolly. This time I was called Jack, and my first week of life as a cab horse was very hard. I had never heard such noise, and the crowds made me feel anxious. But I soon found I could trust my driver and I became used to it.

At least Jerry made a rule to keep Sundays free, when I would be stroked and petted by Lucy and Dolly.

Despite working hard, they were a happy family. But winter came and, after being out in all weathers, Jerry was taken ill.

Although Jerry recovered and, by a stroke of luck, found work as a groom in the country, I had to be sold.

My new master was called Skinner. He was an evil-looking man who ran a low set of cabs. He was hard on the men and the horses. In this place we had no rest day in the heat of summer, and even on the foggy, wet days of winter, he showed us no kindness. Sometimes I was so fevered and worn that I could hardly touch my food.

"I am sure this poor horse cannot take us and all our luggage," said a young girl as we stood at the railway station one day.

"He's alright, miss," said the cab driver, and her father told her to stop making a fuss.

I got along fairly well until we came to Ludgate Hill, but there the heavy load was too much. My feet slipped from under me and I fell heavily to the ground. I heard angry voices, the moving of luggage, and someone said, "He's dead. He'll never get up again."

Cold water was thrown over my head, some was poured into my mouth and slowly I felt my life coming back.

A kind-voiced man was patting me and encouraging me to rise. After one or two attempts, I staggered to my feet. "It's a case of overwork," the farrier told Skinner. "He needs six months' rest."

But after just ten days' rest I was taken to a sale of horses a few miles out of London.

"Poor old fellow. See, grandpa, how he understands kindness." I nuzzled the young boy who was stroking my face.

The farmer with him felt my legs, which were swollen and strained. "He's about fourteen, I should say, Willie. Just trot him out, will you?"

I arched my poor thin neck and threw out my legs as well as I could. "Can't you buy him and make him young again?" Willie pleaded. And so the farmer bought me, just to please his grandson.